A FAMILY HERITAGE BOOK

from the

VERMONT FOLKLIFE

CENTER

The Two Brothers

By

William Jaspersohn

Paintings by

Michael A. Donato

"In memory of my grandparents Carl and Dorothea." —WJ

"For Theresa, Michael-Vincent and Mom, with love." —MD

For information about permission to reproduce
selections from this book, write to

PERMISSIONS
THE VERMONT FOLKLIFE CENTER
MASONIC HALL
3 COURT STREET, BOX 442
MIDDLEBURY, VERMONT 05753

LIBRARY OF CONGRESS | CATALOGING-IN-PUBLICATION DATA

Jaspersohn, William.
    The two brothers / by William Jaspersohn ; paintings by Michael A. Donato.—1st ed.
        p. cm.—(The family heritage series)
    "A family heritage book from the Vermont Folklife Center."
    Summary: Heinrich and Friedrich, two brothers in Prussia in the 1880s, travel
separately to America and end up working on adjacent farms in Vermont.
    ISBN 0-916718-16-6 (hardcover)
    [1. Emigration and immigration—Fiction. 2. German-Americans—Fiction.
3. Farm life—Vermont—Fiction. 4. Brothers—Fiction. 5. Vermont—Fiction.]
    I. Donato, Michael, ill. II. Title. III. Series.
    PZ7.J323 Tw 2000
    [Fic]—dc21   00-024578

ISBN 0-916718-16-6
Printed in China
Distributed by Independent Publishers Group (IPG)
814 North Franklin Street, Chicago, IL 60610

FIRST EDITION

Book design: Joseph Lee, Black Fish Design
Series Editor: William Jaspersohn

10 9 8 7 6 5 4 3 2 1

Publication of this book was made possible by grants from the
Fund for Folk Culture and the **Christian A. Johnson Endeavor Foundation**.

There once were two brothers,

and their names were

Heinrich and Friedrich.

They lived with their mother in a small Prussian town, and they were very, very poor. One day, Heinrich told Friedrich, "I dislike it here in Prussia with its strict laws and pushy soldiers. I have saved just enough money to go to America and seek our fortune. As the youngest, you will stay here with our mother.

When I have found us a home and have steady work, I will
send for both of you. Until then, expect not a word from me.
I shall be busy, but you will both be in my heart."

On a cold day in early spring, Heinrich bid his brother
goodbye and boarded a ship for America.

The crossing was rough and cruel. The gray-green ocean flopped and heaved, and many, including Heinrich, fell ill. There was no doctor anywhere—no nurses either. Three people on board came down with ship fever and died. The ship kept moving. The bodies of the dead were mourned by Heinrich and the others. Then, as is done on ships, the bodies were given to the sea.

Two weeks after it left Prussia, the ship arrived in New York. There, in a customs shed filled with immigrants, an official gave Heinrich a new name.

"You shall be called Henry," the official proclaimed. "It sounds more American than Heinrich, don't you agree? Now, what is your trade?"

In halting English, Henry answered that he'd once been a miller and a farmer.

"Have you a job?" the official asked.

"Nein," replied Henry. In Prussia, "nein" meant "no."

"Good," said the man. "I have one for you. A farmer in Vermont is looking for someone like you to do work for him. Here's a train ticket from him and a dollar for dinner. Go to Grand Central Station. Take the next train to Vermont. We'll wire the farmer that you're coming. Now off with you. Next!"

So, armed with a new name, a ticket and a dollar, Henry made his way to the train station.

There, he boarded an overnight train
that carried him north toward Vermont.

In the morning, Henry awoke to a cold landscape of snow-covered fields and wooded mountains. At the train station, he was met by a plump little man who introduced himself as Farmer Tucker.

"Ja," replied Henry, in his native tongue. "Ich bin Heinrich—er—Henry!"

Mr. Tucker laughed. He drove Henry in a horse-drawn sleigh to his farm, and along the way, he explained to Henry exactly what his duties would be.

There were many duties. Henry didn't mind. He had a job. That was the main thing.

"You'll work hard, but it's hard work in a beautiful place," Mr. Tucker said. "You understand?"

"Ja," replied Henry, thinking of his family. He'd send for them as soon as he'd made enough money.

Life at Tucker Hill Farm was just as Mr. Tucker had described it. In early spring, Henry helped gather maple sap that was boiled into thick, sweet syrup, and when the snow had melted from the fields, he helped with the plowing and planting. He helped deliver the new baby lambs and helped shear the wool from Mr. Tucker's sheep. In the summer, he cut trees for firewood, mended fences, built coops and sheds, and mowed and pitched the hay. In the fall, he helped harvest the corn, oats, barley, potatoes, turnips, carrots, beans and cabbages that he and Mr. Tucker had planted in the spring.

And twice a day, every day, he milked Mr. Tucker's cows. As he milked, he would look through the open barn door at the dark green mountains and think, "I love it here. I have come to the right place."

He saved his wages and learned to read and write
in English. He went to town meetings and celebrated
the American holidays. His favorite was Independence
Day. On that day there was a parade down the main
street of the village, and a brass band played an evening
concert on the village square. When darkness fell,

members of the volunteer fire department touched off
fireworks near the river.

The fireworks excited Henry yet saddened him.
He wished his mother and brother were there to see
them. He still lacked the money for their passage. "I
wonder how they are faring," he thought.

They were not faring well—at least not Henry's dear mother. In the cold of the new year she died of influenza, and Friedrich wept and did not know what to do. In grief, he sold the family's few belongings and, like Henry, purchased a ticket to America. He went by ship. The crossing was rough and cruel.

In New York City, a customs official gave Friedrich a new name.

"It's Frederick," said the official. "Or Fred, if you like."

"Fred." Friedrich smiled. He liked his new name.

"What's your line of work, Fred?" the customs official asked.

When Fred said he'd been a miller and a farmer, the official said, "Wonderful! We'll farm you out. There's a farmer up in Vermont looking for a man with your skills."

"Was ist skills?" asked Fred.

"Never mind," said the man, handing him a train ticket and a dollar for dinner. "Take the next train north. You've got yourself a job, Freddy my boy. Move along, now. Next!"

So, just like his brother before him, Fred took
the next train north.

He didn't know he was traveling toward the place where brother Henry lived. In Vermont, he was greeted by a tall, pleasant-faced farmer named Kew, who drove Fred in a horse-drawn sleigh to his farm.

Now, it so happened that the Kew farm was only one mile from the Tucker farm, where Henry worked. For fifteen months, the two brothers worked within a mile of each other and didn't know it!

Then, one day in April, when the sun had warmed the land and the trees were beginning to bud, Farmer Tucker told Henry to go help mend the fence that ran between the Kew and Tucker farms. "Kew's sending over his hired man," Mr. Tucker added. "He'll give you a hand."

As Henry walked the fence line, he noticed a man approaching in the distance.

Henry rubbed his face and blinked. "Mein Gott," he murmured, "I swear that looks like Friedrich coming, but I know it can't be."

"Heinrich…?" the man called.

"Friedrich?" called Henry, breaking into a run. "Is that you?"

It was. The two men embraced. "I'm Fred now," Friedrich said.

"And I'm Henry."

The two brothers laughed. They cried tears of joy.

"I guess I've come to the right place," Fred said.

"We both have," said Henry, thumping his back. "We both have."

In the years that followed, Henry and Fred bought the Tucker farm from Mr. Tucker, and Henry married and raised a family in its main house. Once in a while, when the winds blew hard and the snow fell sideways, when supper was over and the dishes were cleared, one of Henry's children would say, "Papa, tell us again how you and Uncle Fred came to America." And Henry would laugh and sit back in his chair and begin: "There once were two brothers, and their names were Heinrich and Friedrich...."

Tell Me A Tale

Family stories—often told when different members gather together—serve as an informal family history. Sometimes these tales tell how a relative first came to America and how he or she managed to make a living against difficult odds, or they relate unusual events that may have happened. Such tales are treasured, told over and over, and passed on to younger generations. *The Two Brothers* is an important tale in the Eurich family. It has been passed on to younger kin by Henry's grandsons Clesson and Edward.

Every family has its own tales to tell—your family included. Do this: Ask your grandparents, parents or an older friend to tell you a tale from their past. You and they will enjoy the experience, and some of the tales you hear could be just as amazing as *The Two Brothers!* Later, you might want to retell one of those tales in your own words. You might even want to publish it as a book with your own illustrations. If you do

YOU'LL NEED:
- **pen or pencil**
- **tape recorder (optional)**

1. Draw up a list of five or six questions that you would like to ask a family member. Think up questions that will make the person talk about his or her life. The idea is to get the person talking. Here are some examples:
   - *What was it like when you were growing up?*
   - *What were some of the most memorable things that happened in your childhood?*
   - *As a child, what did you do for fun?*
   - *Did your parents ever tell you stories about their lives, or life before you were born? What were their stories?*
   - *Where did our family come from?*

Think of some more questions and write them down in your notebook.

2. Interview the family member. Choose a quiet place in your house and ask your questions one by one. Listen carefully and write notes in your notebook so that you can remember what the person tells you. If you use a tape recorder, make sure it has a fresh tape in it and that you press RECORD. From time to time, check to make sure the tape recorder is working properly and that you haven't run out of tape.

3. Once you've finished with the interview, go over your notes or the tapes and choose a story to tell in your own words. Then write the story. You might begin with the old tried and true "Once upon a time...." Or you might find a different beginning.

4. Once you've finished writing your story, think about turning it into a finished book with your own illustrations (see the example shown here).

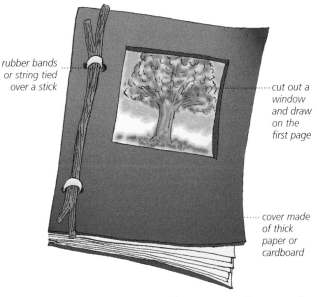

rubber bands or string tied over a stick

cut out a window and draw on the first page

cover made of thick paper or cardboard

No matter how you choose to tell your tale, you should be proud that you have preserved a piece of your own family's heritage!